The Vikings
of Owl Clan

A Seasonaire Story

M A CLARKE

First (and only) Edition

Published by Tekamutt Media 2017

Other books by the author:

Lunaria

The Horizon Conspiracy

www.tekamuttmedia.com

ISBN: 978-0-9929585-6-5

The following is a true story.

The events and characters depicted in this tale are entirely based on real people, whose names and personalities have been (ab)used completely without consent.

It's a nonsensical tale of gibberish, full of obscure references and in-jokes that will make no sense to anybody except the 62 members of Owl Clan, who worked on the Ottawa River during the Summer of 2017.

CONTENTS

Reader discretion is advised. Proceed at your own risk.

CHAPTER ONE

It was midnight on a warm summer's evening in the Ghetto, and Fraser was in his platform having a nightmare. The dreaded Elevator Shaft kept replaying in his mind, and no matter how many times he rafted it, something would always go wrong. After getting smashed in the face by his own paddle for the 12th time, he finally woke up sweating and screaming.

"Argh crikey, mate, it was just a dream. Phew."

And he fell back asleep.

Little did he know, his troubles had only just begun. Because tomorrow at breakfast, he would find out that high water Coliseum was finally in...

CHAPTER TWO

A little while later, Mic-Mack emerged into the light of a full moon from the bowels of a hooligan infested pit of delinquents. She squinted in the dark and managed to read 'Wilderness Tours' on a nearby sign.

"Crap, I have to get back to Owl. I have work in 6 hours!" she slurred to herself.

"This way," said Kaitlyn as she stumbled past, sipping the last dregs of a beer.

Mic-Mack hesitated. She had an itch that needed to be scratched... So she reached up to the sign and began pulling it off its hinges.

"Don't even think about stealing that," Kaitlyn said without looking back.

Mic-Mack froze in mid-reach, waited for Kaitlyn to move a few more steps down the path, then tore the sign off. She had no idea what she was going to do with it, but felt much better having it anyway. She tucked it under an arm and scurried after Kaitlyn in the dark.

CHAPTER THREE

Dirk slept a bit restlessly on nights like this. The Earl of Owl Clan was anxious to see how good his new guides would handle Coliseum at high water. At least he had a few experienced white water experts from around the world like English Gwynn, Scottish Scott, and Imma from New Zealand. She certainly wouldn't take a group of Agouda girls that can't swim down through something as dangerous as Buseater...would she?

He pulled himself out of bed and went to the bathroom. Catching a glimpse of his devastatingly good looks in the mirror was enough to ease his mind, and after having a quick piss, he went back to bed and slept soundly until the morning.

Meanwhile, back in the Ghetto...

CHAPTER FOUR

Taylor woke just as the sun was rising. She rubbed her eyes and looked around, then sighed in relief when she realised she was in her own platform. She'd developed a bad habit of waking up in other people's beds lately, especially if their name began with 'Scotty B', so this immediate discovery was a good omen for her day. Smiling to herself, she donned her double-horned helm, picked up her axe, and made her way to the dining hall where a few of the other members of Owl Clan were already waiting.

CHAPTER FIVE

Owl Clan was made up of four Tribes. There was Office Tribe, who handled rowdy customers and sold ice cream. Ops Tribe liked to think they did all the dirty work that nobody else had the stomach for, but mostly they just walked around a lot. Kitchen Tribe kept everyone fed and therefore happy, especially on fried egg day. And then there was Guide Tribe, supposedly reserved for only the best-looking, most heroic vikings in the clan. They were apparently mighty river warriors who knew no fear... But to be honest, they were all just really good at doing the doggy paddle.

CHAPTER SIX

Kitchen Tribe were busy preparing the clan's breakfast feast, overseen as always by Erin's Iron Fist and Bombaci's Steel Boot. They didn't stand for slacking or thievery, and were known to punish such heinous crimes by seizing control of the clans most precious posession...their beer.

After three years of keeping the clan fed on steak and caesar salads, Alex had taken off her crown of Kitchen Goddess and was now happy to sit back and watch Erin and Bombaci fight over it for the rest of the season. Who would win? Only time will tell.

CHAPTER SEVEN

Guide Tribe were holding their morning meeting. Straun was on the stage addressing a group of new recruits that sat around watching with fearful eyes. He was being loudly energetic as usual, waving a spear around as he spoke.

"When you get to Coliseum, you just have to get up to the bow, look it straight in the eyes and SPEAR THAT DRAGON," he said, dramatically thrusting the spear out towards the crowd, causing several startled yelps.

"A dragon?" Aiden said, exchanging a worried look with Lucy.

"It's okay, I'm pretty sure he's just using a metaphor," Lucy assured him nervously.

Ferrari overheard this and turned to them both. "Yeah, a metaphor. Of course..." Then he looked quickly away again.

CHAPTER EIGHT

As the clan ate breakfast, KT recounted the tale of how she once led an Esprit raiding party across the river to pillage Owl Clan's store of granola. Under the cover of darkness, KT and her former clanmates landed on Owl Beach carrying swords, shields and clubs. She led the raid directly into the garage (where Owl kept all of their best weapons like mops and brooms).

As she kicked in the door she was greeted with an unexpected sight. A handsome kiwi known as Hadleigh was already there, adjusting a battering ram, and when he took one look at the fearsome viking warrior and her two handed battle-axe, her face streaked with war-paint and a voice that could be mistaken for thunder, he knew she had to be his.

So Hadleigh took up his hammer and slew the rest of the raiding party in a flurry of carnage and KT was so impressed that she dropped her axe, took Hadleigh in her arms and carried him upstairs into the Ritz attic, where they tore off each other's clothes, found an old mattress and...and...

"And that's the true story of how Rhys was conceived," KT said and peaced out.

CHAPTER NINE

Each Tribe was assigned a different weapon. The Office carried axes, Ops carried hammers and Guides carried spears (the Kitchen Tribe used whatever cooking utensil happened to be in their hand at the time).

The exception to this rule was Big Ben. Why was he called Big Ben, you ask? Was he named after the size of his enormous.....paddle? His mouth? His personality? While all of these things were remarkably Big, he was in fact named after his gigantic age. At 29, he was one of the elders at Owl Clan, and so many of the underlings would mistakenly come to him for advice and wisdom. What they usually got in return was an entertainingly offensive or sarky comment.

So, while the rest of Guide Tribe armed themselves with spears, Ben carved himself a giant wooden spoon, which he used to stir shit whenever an opportunity presented itself.

CHAPTER TEN

The English writer Matt found himself in Ops Tribe and was trying his best to learn all the weird river lingo so that he could join in the other vikings' conversations. It was complicated, to say the least. Not to mention filthy. These people were obsessed with punching through each other's' holes, surfing on tongues, swamping, boofing, going hard forward and sometimes even harder backwards, flipping, spinning, and Matt's personal favourite, thunder dunking, whatever the shit that meant.

So far, amid all this bewildering sexual innuendo, all he'd managed to decipher was that some bloke called Eddie was loose somewhere on the river. He had to be a dangerous criminal or something because everyone wanted to catch him. So Matt decided he would try and earn the respect of his fellow clanmates and catch Eddie himself.

CHAPTER ELEVEN

After breakfast, Gaston the illegal Mexican immigrant began his long shift in the kitchen. It was his job to peel carrots, chuck corn, mop floors and wash dishes. Occasionally, he was trusted to do these same tasks on the Owl Longboat Pontoon.

Gaston couldn't help feeling that he wasn't being used to his full potential. After all, he was a highly experienced burrito chef, taco maker and sushi expert. As well as this, he was a professional love guru, a famous movie director, a scholar, an astronaut, the best poker player in the West, a champion horseback rider, he invented the screw-top bottlecap, he could recite over a hundred decimals of Pi, he could shoot a beer can from a mile away (blindfolded), he spoke 17 different languages and he learned how to roll a kayak on his first day. (One of these facts is actually true, but the rest only exist within the wild jungle of his imagination).

As he was chopping an onion in the kitchen, his superhuman ears heard a noise coming from outside. Someone was screaming. He took up his kitchen knife and ran outside, declaring loudly, "Fear not, Gaston will save you!"

CHAPTER TWELVE
(intoxicated)

So Gaston the illegals Mexican immigrant ran outside with his kitchen knife and saw Liam wrestling 7 chipmunks who were trying to steal the staff lunch. "aaaagh!!!" screamed liam and Gaston ran in to save him using his ninja powers. And it worked. He saved lunch and Liam was all "thanks man. I was so needing help right there but you saved me. Thank you.'" And Gaston said" it is my pleasure. You are bold sire."

"i know," said liam. And then the chapter ended coz Matt was drunking and needed to dance some more.

CHAPTER THIRTEEN

As a crowd of Owlies gathered to watch the spectacle of Liam and Gaston fighting a bunch of chipmunks, Claudia took her moment to sneak into the kitchen while nobody was looking. As the matriarch of Owl Clan, Claudia could carry out acts of psychological warfare whenever she wanted, and nobody dared to oppose her. So she took full advantage of her power.

When she wasn't kidnapping members of Ops Tribe to force them into weeding her gardens, she liked to perform mischievous pranks. Last week, she hid all of the breakfast hash browns so nobody could find them and this morning she decided to swap all of the chocolate chip muffins with blueberry cupcakes instead. With this latest jape completed, she snuck back out of the kitchen and retreated into the wilds to await her next opportunity to torment her employees.

She is also a really nice person and a joy to work for.

#pleasedontfireme

CHAPTER FOURTEEN

Regan and Marianne were in the Owl Store dealing with a very irritating viking customer that didn't really know what he wanted and kept asking silly questions.

"No, sir, we can't guarantee that you won't get wet on the river," Marianne explained patiently.

"You might die, too," Regan added helpfully.

"Regan!" Marianne whispered. "You can't say it like that!"

"Well its true," Regan said.

"What about lunch?" said the customer. "I'm allergic to everything except roast lobster."

"Umm..." the two girls said, not sure what to say to him.

Sensing the hesitation, Bootstrap Vinnie descended from the ceiling covered in dripping seaweed and with a small beaver clinging to his head.

"Sorry sir, we don't have roast lobster," Vinnie said apologetically. "But chef Nolan cooks a fine steak BBQ. Would that satisfy you?"

"Oh yes," smiled the customer. "That would be most excellent."

"Can I be of any more assistance?" Bootstrap Vinnie asked. The beaver winked.

"No thank you," said the customer.

"Thanks Bootstrap Vinnie!" Marianne and Regan said in unison.

And with that, Bootstrap Vinnie ascended once

again and disappeared into the office ceiling, where he dwelled for all eternity, always ready to answer any Owl related questions.

CHAPTER FIFTEEN

Nick Flemming, AKA Flemmingo, AKA The Saltiest Boy Alive, was late for work again. He was driving his goat wagon down the road, but was stuck behind a donkey going 2kph, which made him feel grumpy. He lived with his parents because he wasn't old enough to stay on Owl Clan's property, and this also made him grumpy. So did the weather. And hippies. Also liberals. Asians. Raft guides. Raft guides driving the walker. Communists. The elderly. The young. The middle aged. Mexicans. Being told what to do. Doing work. People that wear jackets. I could go on, because there's not actually a single thing in life that Flemmingo doesn't complain about.

As he pulled into Owl Lane, his goat was able to move into second gear and he sped down the lane towards the Clan grounds. He almost ran over Mic-Mack and Kaitlyn, who hadn't made it back from WT yet. Mic-Mack seemed to be carrying a large sign with her.

"Hey Nick!" she shouted as he passed by. "Give us a ride! We're so late."

Reluctantly, Nick pulled over his goat wagon and let the two girls climb aboard. Giving people rides also made Flemmingo very grumpy. And so did being called Flemmingo. Poor Nick. Going through puberty is tough, even for vikings.

CHAPTER SIXTEEN
(Guest chapter written by the women of Owl Clan (But mostly Mic-Mack))

It was a dark and stormy night (#butwasitthough) and the clan women were sitting around the fire discussing matters of wine and cheese.

Suddenly, out of the forest emerged Mik Mak holding a large sign. Kaitlyn came swiftly after muttering and swearing under her breath. Mik Mak grabbed her engraving tools and started quickly etching in the firelight. The women looked on fascinated. An entrancing glow emerged from the clearing as she worked her magic.

Suddenly, Mik Mak's eyes went white as a streak of lightning shot straight into the sky, clearing the clouds and showing her deepest desire. Written in the stars was one clear phrase:

"Matt, will you go to prom with me?"

#MikMattProm2017

CHAPTER SEVENTEEN

T-Roy stretched and had a big satisfying yawn. He sat up in his cosy bed and hummed a little song to himself. Today was his day off, and he had big plans. You see, T-Roy is one of those wee Hobbits from New Zealand and hobbits love nothing more than going on whimsical adventures.

So T-Roy got up, packed a little knapsack full of snacks, put on his little hobbit sized jacket, and his tiny little boots, then set off down the lane, thinking about all the wonderful things he might see. He skipped along the road merrily waving to everyone he saw, and people stopped and said "Look! There goes little T-Roy, off on one of his adventures!"

Little T-Roy was in for a big surprise that day. He had no idea of the terrible danger he was walking into, as he made his way into the bush, walking alongside the river...

CHAPTER EIGHTEEN

Guide Tribe loaded all of the rafts onto the wagon and Gus danced through it all. He always danced wherever he went. He was probably the best dancer in Owl Clan, and would always have his arms and legs pumping to the rhythm of a song that only he could hear. Even in the bedroom, it's been told...

The ox-drawn wagon set off, towing all of the boats, and the Trip B guides sat together in the back. Gus continued to dance even in his seat.

"Where did you learn those funky moves Gus?" Evelyn asked him inquisitively. She was also rather into dancing, and wanted to pick up some tips from the energetic Scotsman.

"What do you mean?" Gus said, thrusting his arms out in a fancy wave.

"You are dancing again," said Maris, sitting opposite. "Right now!"

"Oh, you mean this?" Gus said, churning an invisible bowl of ice cream with both hands. "This isn't dancing. This is just the way my people stay warm. You have no idea how cold it gets in Scotland , guys."

"Uhh, I think we do. We're Canadian," Tanner pointed out.

The wagon pulled into the put-in, and Nick St Pierre parallel parked the oxen with the skill of a man who rafts so very often.

They put the boats into the river, and shit got real...

CHAPTER NINETEEN

Shaggy Gwyn was the most experienced viking on the Ottawa, and his knowledge of its twists and turns were unparalleled among the community. He'd recently suffered a nasty injury when a paddle caught him in the eye, so now he wore an eyepatch and spoke exactly like a pirate for his safety speech. He still used all the same jokes, though. At the end he turned to his rafters and said, "Aye, mateys, its time to make a sacrifice to the river Gods. Any volunteers?"

Nobody replied.

"Thought not. In that case... Eenie, meanie, minie, mo..." His finger landed on Myriam.

It was Myriam's last day at Owl Clan... The French-speaking viking girl from Kitchen Tribe had decided to come rafting one last time, and had unfortunately ended up in the team leader's raft.

Without hesitation, the rafters tipped Myriam out of the boat.

"Why me!?" she asked as she floated helplessly.

"Yargh, hard forwards ye sea dogs!" barked Gwyn, steering his boat away from the danger zone.

Bubbles appeared around poor Myriam. The water began to ripple and foam, and suddenly rising like a mythical monster, because it is a mythical monster, came the Loch Ness Monster! Nessie was on holiday from Scotland and was visiting the area with one of those 2-year working holiday visas. Commonwealth privileges and all that. She'd gotten a breezy summer job on the Ottawa as the First River God, and wouldn't let Owl Clan pass without a human sacrifice.

"Aaaagh!" Myriam cried as Nessie loomed over her, examining her offering. Myriam must have looked delicious, because Nessie opened her jaws wide, leaned down, plucked her out of the water, and swallowed her whole.

"Yum yum," said Nessie. "Tastes like maple syrup." And she disappeared again beneath the water.

And so Owl Clan's eventful day on the river had begun, and they had lost their first member... Safe travels, Myriam... See you in Valhalla.

CHAPTER TWENTY

"You just wouldn't BELIEVE how many times Nick St Pierre goes rafting.

He rafts often.

CHAPTER TWENTY-ONE OR SOMETHING
(intoxicated – Post-Portage)

So we are on some bus in Quebec portagtoes. It went well for some. There was dancing. There was drinking. There was making out...for some. All in all, I'd say it was a pretttu good night of partying viking style.

Karma happened. Skinny dipping was involved. Did betrayals get betrayed? Lol maybe or maybe not. All I know is that Matt, he danced for his life. As did we all.

O am so very hammered that this won't make enahye sense will it ai and so flemmingo and Fraser and Evelyn and Taylor and Kaitlyn and liam and Hannah and Micky a cling ton and Nolan, Nolan, Nolan on the river, I said Nolan, Nolan, Nolan on the river was in the back of the bus, and we went all the way to the Owl Clan base camp on the Ottawa river of rivers. The only river. Yes. Bit drunk. But I love you all. I do. Best summer ever. Eh? Eh? Say yes. Its true.

This is matt, clarkie, me, saying goodnight ai revoir, auf vedersein and good night.

To beeeeee in the process of continuation....

PS then we walked down the road, motxh was cold, troy was a hobbit mark was mark, the corn was glowing a serene shade of moonlighted moon. I love

the moon. We walked until we stopped. The end.
    To still be contined...
Pretty sure this mess is a succcccessfuk summary of
Portal. Portage. A royal mess

CHAPTER TWENTY-TWO

Where were we? Oh yeah... After a shocking immersion-breaking tangent involving lots of alcohol, we find ourselves back on the Ottawa River. It's a beautiful sunny morning, the Clan is in high spirits (despite just witnessing Myriam get devoured by a giant mythical water lizard) and the guides set a course for the first challenge of the day... McKoys.

"Easy forward!" said Squid to his rafters. They responded by tentatively waggling their paddles against the water's surface.

Oh not again, Squid thought to himself. *Another bunch of lazy punters who are scared of getting their hands wet.* "Okay let's try second gear!" he said, even though they were still on the flat. He just had to see what they considered to be "80% effort". The group of middle-class vikings from Toronto did at least submerge their paddles this time, but pulled with the combined effort of a small mouse.

The raft drifted towards the roaring rapids, and Squid tried his best to line them up properly, but it was no good.

"Please paddle guys! Hard forwards!!!" he cried in vain. At sight of the approaching waves, the clients had decided to "hold on in fear" instead. They drifted hopelessly to the right side of the river... much too far. They were heading straight towards a nasty pool of swirling water created by the bones of some long-dead dinosaur that called himself Phil. The churning water gaped wide like the jaws of a hungry animal.

As Squid's raft hit the wrong side of Phil's Hole, the boat tipped up and over, spilling everyone, including Squid. He fell overboard in his trademark display of flailing limbs, and Phil's Hole sucked everyone in.

And then the piranhas came.

CHAPTER TWENTY-THREE

Scotty B perched on a very fine rock to sit and watch the carnage unfold. This was his favourite part of the job as one of Owl Clan's official Viking Artists. He took out his stone tablet, hammer and chisel, and began carving a rudimentary image of rafts manoeuvring through McKoys, skirting Phil's Hole, and of course Squid's clients being eaten by piranhas. He worked quickly and efficiently, his fingers blurring as they swiftly created a work of art. Any punters who survived their day on the river would surely buy a copy of this later as a souvenir.

Then he spotted Maris, heroically tossing her throwbag towards Squid in an effort to save him from the deadly school of snapping fish.

"Oh my sweet darling!" cried Scotty B in awe. How brave his woman was, a true shieldmaiden of the Clan. He admired the way she straddled the wooden thwarts for support as she pulled Squid out of the hole and hauled him to safety. Scotty B turned to his tablet once again and etched the goddess-like image of Maris saving Squid into his stone, before crying "It is done! My masterpiece!" And he kissed it. Such is the life of a videokayak-- I mean Viking Artist.

CHAPTER TWENTY-FOUR?
(intoxicated – Basement Ball)

So..........

On the Ottawa River today. There was a ball. A ballsiest ball of balls. In the basement. And I made a vow to be the last person in the ball. And I succeeded.

It seemed that basement ball was a success. Because I saw people making out and dancing and making promises they could never keep in such an intoxicated state. But it happened anyway. And that is what is meant to happen in a ball.

Mickmack, I dont know where you are but I'm glad you invited me to my first ball because in school I wasn't cool enough to go and noone asked me but this time you did and I had fun :D

Omg anyway. Enough lovey dovey stuff, we were rafting on the Ottawa river and the next rapid was HORSEAHOE BABY FACE DUSE! WHAT HAPPENED TUERE ATAY TUNED TO FIND OUT IN TUE NDT EXCITIBG IBSTQLLMENT OF AN OWL ATORY CHAPTER 24 THE TIME WHEN SMEONE ELSE FALLS IN AND HAS TO FIGHT A SHARK!!!

CHAPTER TWENTY-FIVE
(Live reading at the Owl Talon Show)

After the piranha's had finished devouring most of Squid's clients, the trip continued downstream, stopping to surf on a baby's face. That sounds worse than it is, because it's actually just the name of a rapid which is famous for making clients (and guides) scream like a baby.

This rapid proved to be more fun for the sport rafts, because the big boats could just roll right over it. The clan had argued over what to call these "big boats" for many days and nights, until eventually Dirk settled the argument by pitting several guides to a wrestling match, with the winner being allowed to give the boats whatever name they wanted. This was a good plan, foiled only by the fact that the winner of the brawl had lost most of their brain cells during the fight, so the most imaginative name they could come up with for these big boats was... Big Boats.

As the guides continued down the river, Kitchen Tribe was busy preparing lunch, the second most important part of the day. The kitchen was a beehive of activity as each member performed their daily task - Sid was responsible for chasing away chipmunks and seagulls, because she took it upon herself to make sure they all survived. Using her vegan powers, she can often be seen leading a train of chipmunks down the lane and setting them free in the woods, like a less creepy version of the pied piper.

Nolan was seasoning a hundred steaks, unaware whether he was awake or dreaming. His dreams lately had become very similar to his days, and he often found himself dreaming about meat, or if he was having a nightmare, scary thoughts of customers asking for their steaks to be served well-done.

Elsewhere in the kitchen, Captain Kat ran around in an ever increasing level of panic as the day went on, and Alex was examining a bowel of leftovers from 3 days ago, weighing up whether anyone would notice if she added a bit of extra sauce and reheated it. It was a better alternative than spending the next 5 hours kneading pizza dough again for those ungrateful base-dwellers.

Meanwhile, over in the office, Margaret was manning the carrier pigeon tower, waiting for a message from Trip B to confirm they had made it to the put-in. She was pondering how it would be better to invent some kind of long-distance gadget that could send and receive messages via invisible magic airwaves, when a pigeon arrived carrying a bloodstained note. She plucked the note off the leg, and unrolled it. She read it aloud to herself, and as she did, her eyes bulged wider in terror.

In giant capital letters, the note read "SEND HELP NOW! MONSTERS EATING PEOPLE. MYRIAM GONE. PIRANHA'S IN PHILS HOLE! SHARK!!!" This final word trailed off in a bloodstain and the rest was unreadable.

Margaret threw down the note and scrambled down the tower. She found Dirk and explained the situation. Only one man could save his clanspeople now - it was time to summon Thor.

CHAPTER TWENTY-SIX

Dirk and Margaret went over to the riverside firepit which was where they performed all of their sacrificial rituals. It was a circle of giant stone boulders which Dirk had hauled out of the river using his bare hands and planted in a comfortable seating arrangement around a big hole.

"Okay Margaret, in order to summon Thor, I need you to bring me a spoon, a bowl and the loudest, most muscular, most fearsomely intimidating member of Owl Clan that you can find."

"Got it," said Margaret. She came back 5 minutes later with the spoon, a bowl, and Hannah.

"You asked for me?" she squeaked, unsure what Dirk had in mind.

"Yes, we need a human sacrifice to summon Thor," Dirk explained, and armed himself with the spoon.

"Wait a minute!" Margaret interrupted. "This is 1017, isn't it a bit socially insensitive to perform ritualistic sacrifices in this day and age without consent?"

"You're right," Dirk agreed. "Hannah, do you mind if we use you as a human sacrifice?"

"Honestly, I'd rather you didn't," she said.

So they did it the politically correct way, which was inoffensive and vague, with Dirk chanting gibberish at the sky and waving his arms a bit, until the Gods above responded.

A sudden rush of storm clouds spiralled overhead as lightning streaked across the sky and booming thunder split the air, deafeningly loud. A bright glowing orb shot down out of the sky. It careened towards the ground at a hundred miles an hour and crashed into the grass next to the fire pit. The orb glowed white hot, then began to cool, turning from white to red, to a tanned skin colour as it took on the form of a mighty warrior. A godlike being from the heavens, he carried a hammer and his long golden hair flowed around his face in a veil of silken majesty. Thor looked up, slung the hammer over one shoulder and gave Dirk and Margaret a warm, happy smile.

"Right on, guys. S'up?" he said.

CHAPTER TWENTY-SEVEN

Easton the viking intern had managed to find his way into each of the various Tribes of Owl Clan, and learn all of their secrets. This made him arguably the most powerful member of the Clan, as he could singlehandedly bring the whole place to its knees in a devilish plan of blackmail...if he so desired. You see, Easton knew where the kitchen tribe kept all of the best leftovers (including the super-secret gluten-free cake stash). His time with Ops taught him which cabins provided the best cover for a sneaky nap. And Office Tribe were forced to let him know the combination to the big vault where they were allowed to take 5 minute breaks every hour just to roll around in the mountains of hundred dollar bills.

So with all this insider knowledge, Easton had planted a bullseye on his back. There were certain people who would pay a pretty price for the things he knew. And some would even kill for it... Easton hadn't yet noticed the prying eyes, watching him from the shadows, waiting to strike...

He didn't know it yet, but Easton's days at Owl Clan were numbered...

CHAPTER TWENTY-EIGHT

It was Skylar who discovered the body. She was enjoying an otherwise pleasant day off, taking a stroll around the boardwalk and heading for the beach when out of the corner of her eye, she looked up and saw Easton dangling from the big viking mast.

"Is that...? Oh, god, it is! Um, oh man, this is bad, um, shiiit." She was a bit lost for words as you can tell.

She climbed up the mast for a closer look.

"Huuurgh," gurgled Easton. Skylar's heart jumped and she nearly fell off. He's alive!

"Easton!" she cried. "What happened? Who did this to you!?"

"Hooligans... Delinquents..." Easton mumbled these final 2 words and then went silent.

"Easton? Easton? EASSTOOOON!!!" Skylar shook him a bit but it was no good. Easton had departed Owl Clan forever. (Or maybe until next summer)

Anyway, what could he have meant by those last 2 words? Hooligans and delinquents. They were extravagant words for someone on his deathbed, not to mention mysteriously mysterious... Skylar didn't understand, but upon closer inspection, she saw that Easton had a message tied around his neck. The message was written on a broken paddle, carved into the wood with a knife. It read: WE NO WOT U

DUN. GIV IT BAK IN 1 HOUR, OR ELSE...

Whoever wrote such a message was clearly either drunk or uneducated, because of all the terrible spelling mistakes. But one thing Skylar felt sure of...this was a threat. And she didn't like threats. Not one bit. She had to decipher its meaning and figure out what to give back, and to who, before something else bad happened! And she only had 1 hour to do it!

Now time is moving pretty slowly in this story (maybe you noticed we haven't even gone past McKoys yet, and it's not even lunchtime on the base) and so there's actually at least a week or 2 before this particular story thread needs to get resolved.

Still...who could be behind this terrible mysterious murder, and threatening message? I certainly don't know.

CHAPTER TWENTY-NINE

The trip continued down river, leaving McKoys behind and paddling along a pleasant bit of flatwater that wasn't infested with monsters, sharks or piranhas. They passed by a grassy bank on their left, which had a pole sticking out of the water beside it. A man had been tied to this pole by a series of ropes around his arms, legs and waist. He could not move, and seemed to have numerous lines across his belly, indicating various water levels. Right now, the water was just above the man's belly. He glared at the boats as they drew near, his eyes wide and slightly insane.

Trip leader Gwyn pulled out his spyglass and peered through it with his good eye. "Aye mateys, just as I thought! Ye olde water level is riding high!"

"Um, who is that?" asked one of the clients.

"Who? Gauge-Man? Why, that's the way we see how high the water level is, yargh," said Gwyn, still speaking like a pirate.

"But why is he tied to a pole?" the client asked again, sounding quite concerned.

"He's the longest-running member of Owl Clan," explained Ferrari, hanging his head low. "When you've worked here for as long as he has, you go a bit loony. Dirk and Claudia don't have the heart to fire people, though, so they always find something useful for you to do..."

A respectful silence fell over the expedition at this

point. Everyone knew that Ferrari was next to take over as Gauge-Man. It was just a matter of time.

They threw Gauge-Man a corn on the cob, and he snatched it out of the air and started gnawing on it noisily. And then on they paddled.

They came to the next rapid of their journey. Some called it The Lorne. Others knew it as Black Chute... Either way, this was one mean rapid, made up of several large waves including the infamous Wagon-Eater, a wave so big...yes, it could eat a wagon.

So could the monster that lurked beneath the surface of the flatwater at the top. As the flotilla approached, a giant scaly body rose up out of the water, dripping and revealing a grin of razor sharp teeth. It had the body of a walrus, the head of a crocodile, and it towered above the terrified Owl Clan vikings over a hundred feet tall.

"Greetings!" the monster snarled, flapping its surprisingly tiny arms in a welcoming gesture. "I am the Second River God. I've been expecting you."

CHAPTER THIRTY

"Another one!" cried Holly in despair. She'd seen enough monsters for one trip, and this one had a lot of teeth, which was worrying.

"Fear not, my sheila!" said Tim, leaping onto his beloved's boat in a graceful jump and twirling his spear above his head in a flourish. "I seen worse than this fella back home. He's just a croc! Watch me turn him into a nice leather handbag for you, darling!"

Tim ran down the length of Holly's Big Boat, jabbed the butt of his spear into the front and pole-vaulted towards the giant Croco-Walrus River God thing.

The monster watched this with amusement. Tim flew through the air semi-heroically, but realised at the last minute that he was not actually tall enough to pose any real threat to the enormous beast. Tim jabbed the spear into its belly button before bouncing harmlessly off and landing in the river with a small splash.

The River God smirked and shook its head. "A bit cocky and desperate to put his spear in another person's orifice. He must be Australian."

"Let us pass!" demanded Holly as she fished her little Timmy out of the water.

"All right, all right," said the Walrus-Croc. "I'll let you go... if you can answer my riddle."

"A riddle?" said Fraser, raising one eyebrow.

Riddles were his guilty pleasure. And here was an opportunity to prove himself useful on the river as more than just someone who falls out a lot. He leaned forwards eagerly and listened.

"Riddle me this," said the River God. "What is the difference between a cupcake and a muffin?"

CHAPTER THIRTY-ONE

"It's to do with size, right?"

"Yeah muffins are bigger."

"I've seen a big cupcake before, though."

"Then it was a muffin..."

"Size doesn't matter, it's all about the icing."

"Yes, only cupcakes can have icing."

"I've put icing on a muffin before."

"You blasphemous swine!"

"Cupcakes come in those little paper things."

"So do muffins..."

"Not always!"

"Is it a sweet and savoury question?"

"You eat muffins at breakfast."

"Not English muffins you idiot!"

"It's definitely about the icing..."

"No, it's the dough mixture."

"It depends how long you cook them for."

"No it doesn't!"

"I think you'll find that muffins are actually a type of bread."

"As if!"

The Walrus Croc River God listened to all of this in dumbstruck silence, amazed at how much thought these vikings had put into the silly question. He decided to agree to whatever the next person said.

"Muffins are just better..."

"YES!" cried the River God, bellowing over

everyone, making the clan finally shut up. "He's right, that weirdo in the bushes. Muffins ARE just better. That's the only difference. Now go on you lot, get out of here. You've given me a right headache." And with that, the giant Walrus Croc plunged underwater and disappeared in a pool of bubbles.

The clan turned towards the bushes to see who had given them the answer. They saw Matt crouching down, half hidden, but not very well.

"Shh," he whispered. "I'm trying to catch Eddie."

Then, after a moment, he added, "You haven't seen him, have you?"

CHAPTER THIRTY-TWO

"Who could have done such a horrible thing!?" cried Marianne when Skylar told them all about Easton.

"I bet it was one of those dirty Ops people," said Regan, scrunching up her nose in disgust.

"Why would you say that!?" said Taylor, deeply offended, because her beloved Nick worked in Ops. She didn't like to think about him getting his hands all covered in filth down some smelly toilet, but facts were facts, and that is exactly what Nick has to do every day before he is allowed to visit her and use those same hands for other things.

"Don't you get it?!" cried Mik-Mack. "This is exactly what they want! Whoever did this wants us to turn on each other. It's what I would do if I were them…"

"You sound like you know who it was!" said Skylar.

"It is kinda obvious…" Mik-Mack said. "Hooligans? Delinquents? Easton's last words, remember? Plus the message on his neck is asking for us to 'give it back'…" Mik-Mack held up a large sign. "I think Wilderness Tours Clan are upset about me stealing this."

"But they killed Easton!" Regan said. "Don't you think that's a bit of an overreaction, even for them?"

"I might have stolen a keg too…" Mik-Mack said

sheepishly. "And a few chairs. And I found a collection of WT paddles in my platform which weren't there before last week's Rafters party... So I probably stole those too."

"No wonder they're mad!" said Margaret. "Well, we need to prepare. They're gonna be here in 45 minutes. We have to be ready!"

"Let's set some traps!" said Regan excitedly.

They agreed, picked up their axes and all walked outside. But as soon as they did, a spear came flying out of the woods towards them.

Regan didn't even have time to duck. It caught her in the chest and she fell over backwards very dead.

"There!!!" shouted Marianne, pointing towards the trees. A young viking wearing a WT helm was running across the wagon parking lot and into the Ghetto. "After him!!!"

The Office Owlies ran after him and chased him into the cornfield. They left poor Regan behind, who had seen her final day at Owl Clan, and joined Myriam and Easton in the never ending Viking Rave that was Valhalla.

CHAPTER THIRTY-THREE

Little T-Roy was merrily skipping through the forest having a gay old time, singing songs, dancing with blue jays, and his happy smile shone brighter than the sun. He reached the river just before noon, and decided to find a spot to sit and have his picnic. So, on a high cliff overlooking the rather scary sounding Butcher's Knife rapid, the little Hobbit stopped to eat his lunch.

He didn't hear the footsteps creeping up behind him as he laid his blanket on the ground...

And he didn't see the glint of steel reflecting off the sun behind him as he took out his sandwiches...

And it wasn't until it was too late that he felt the breath on the back of his neck...

Someone jumped on him. "Gotcha!!"

"AAIIIIEEE!" shrieked little T-Roy.

"Bahahaha! You should see your face!" the attacker said.

T-Roy turned around in his shaking little boots. Then his terror melted away. "Why it's you! Where did you come from, Ariana, my fellow New Zealand Hobbit friend, and occasional beer thief?"

"I followed you! You always have the bist adventures little T-Roy with your little Hobbit jacket and tiny Hobbit socks."

They laughed and Ariana joined the picnic and they talked longingly of home, and sang songs of their

47

people and did a bunch of other whimsical Hobbity things.

Then a giant snake's head loomed out of the river and peered at them from the edge of the cliff. It was a River God, and the Hobbits' noisy merriment had awoken him. He looked extremely pissed off.

"How dare you wake me?" the River Snake hissed.

Little T-Roy and little Ariana both jumped. "Oh no! A monster!"

"I suppose you're going to challenge us with a riddle?" asked T-Roy.

"Or sacrifice us to the river?" said Ariana.

"No, actually," said the humungous snake. "I'm just going to eat you." He opened his big jaws wide and the 2 little hobbits stared into the maw of death.

Something awoke inside little T-Roy. A terrible wrath he had never felt before. His face contorted into a fierce scowl, his eyes bulged, he stuck his tongue out and stomped his feet and pumped his arms, breaking into one mean haka wardance.

Then he grabbed his spear and roared "TEEROOOOY JEEENKINS!!" and threw himself at the monster. Ariana did not hesitate to join him.

CHAPTER THIRTY-FOUR

Alex stared at her empty fridge and despaired. Someone had forgotten to go hunting and so there was nothing to cook for the clan's dinner.

"Well, shit," she muttered to herself. If she wasn't slaving away all day making the same 7 meals once a week, she was put into ridiculous situations like this where she'd have to go out into the wild and catch some friggin food.

"Time to be a hero again..." Then an idea struck her. "Wait, we already have a hero!"

This was met with silence.

"I said I need a Heroux to save the day!" she said louder.

Still nothing.

"Dammit, Emily, get over here!" she yelled.

"What's up Alex?" Heroux said, appearing from around the corner.

"We have no dinner. You need to assemble a team and go out to the river and hunt us something to cook. Be the hero we need Heroux."

"Okay!" said Heroux the hero , giving a little viking salute.

She gathered a whole bunch of Owl kitchen staff, including Brie, Steff, Gaston, Liam, Nolan (on the river), Kat, Paige, and Second Brie, also known as Jordan.

They set out immediately, which was good because

otherwise kitchen Tribe would be left back at base forever and would never get to join in with the rest of the absurd monster hunting and crazy adventuring that everyone else was up to in this nonsensical story.

CHAPTER THIRTY-FIVE

Even after the Clan had navigated Black Chute without falling into the mighty Wagon-Eater, Colin could still hear screaming. It didn't seem to be coming from any of the rafters, so he wondered for a moment if he was going mad.

"Can anyone else hear that?" he asked, in his deadpan voice reserved for when he is either making a sarcastic joke, or when he is worried that he's going mad...

"I can," said Tanner, glancing nervously downstream. Somewhere out of sight, a high pitched wail echoed into the sky. Tanner had heard clients make such a noise, shortly before they were sucked into the bowels of Coliseum. But this was a different noise. "That sounds like a Hobbit fighting a giant River Snake..." he decided.

"You mean there's more of these things?!" cried Lucy. Her hand instinctively went to her shoulder, which had a habit of dislocating at the first sign of danger. It was very inconvenient.

"There's nothing for it, we have to keep going!" said Naomi, mildly annoyed by the delay. It was just a giant boat-eating snake monster, after all.

The Clan paddled on, until they arrived at Butcher's Knife rapid shortly after the screaming had ceased. It was like paddling into an abattoir. Blood and chunky pieces of meat were littered all across the razor sharp rock face on the right side of the river, as if someone had cheese-grated the world's biggest steak. Far above, sitting on the top of the cliff was a giant decapitated snakes head and two small Hobbits. They were covered from head to toe in blood, and were both eating sandwiches.

"Oh look, it's our big friends," said Ariana, jumping to her feet and giving the Clan a cheerful wave.

"Hi guys!" said T-Roy, jumping up next to her and grinning happily.

"What the hell happened here guys?" Tanner said, his mouth dangling wide open.

"We're having a picnic! It's such a lovely day, don't you think?" said T-Roy.

"No, no, no, no..." said Lucy, shaking her head rapidly. She pointed at the dismembered snake's head dangling from an overhanging tree branch. "What happened to THAT?"

Ariana and T-Roy's grins faded in an instant and they glared down at the clan. "Let's just say, he swam right..." said T-Roy.

That didn't really make any sense, but neither T-Roy nor Ariana was apparently not going to elaborate further, and they simply continued to death-stare the clan until they had drifted downriver out of sight.

CHAPTER THIRTY-SIX
(mildly intoxicated – Post-Baseball)

The Clan paddled on, continuing their surprisingly eventful day on the Ottawa River. Usually, there weren't any sea monsters, piranhas, sharks or human sacrifices (that last part isn't technically true), and frankly it was turning into a trip they would never forget.

Then a bunch of WT boats came around the corner, being rowdy as usual, and challenged the Owlies to a game of River Baseball. Of course the Clan agreed, despite having a whole bunch of foreign fools who didn't even know how to play on their team.

As they made their way across the flatwater, Owl pitched ball after ball at the WT batters, who skillfully whacked each one far into the trees on the shore, scoring many home runs. Basically, they all took the game way too seriously, and Owl Clan laughed at their macho over-confidence and non-subtle dick-measuring.

Then something miraculous happened. Something nobody could have predicted.

Owl pitched a ball towards the WT batter, who swung like a champion and hit it high into the air towards the trees. The Owlies groaned, and watched in mild boredom as the ball sailed towards the shoreline, where it would obviously be yet another home run.

Then, out of the bushes came an Australian voice, a master heckler who said something scathing and offensive that made all of the WT fools really grumpy. Nobody could even see Mitch until he stepped out from the treeline, covered in camouflage and wearing a big glove. He casually walked forwards and plucked the ball out of the air and won the game.

Everyone cheered. It was the greatest sporting moment of the century, one that you could never write, because nobody would believe it. But it happened. I was there.

CHAPTER THIRTY-SEVEN

Several things happened next.

In the cornfield, Office Tribe caught up to their quarry and wrestled the murderous fiend to the ground.

"You killed Regan!!!" Marianne yelled in his face, grabbing him by his shirt and shaking him.

"I'm sorry! Please don't hurt me! They made me do it!" the young lad pleaded.

"Who made you do it?" demanded Taylor, looming over him as he lay on the ground. She held her axe close to his nose to show she meant business.

"Wilderness Clan!" he cried, bursting into tears. "They told me to get revenge for stealing their sign. I didn't mean to cause so much trouble! Honest I didn't, I'm just a stupid boy with no brains who likes to swim down the river completely alone and not tell anybody. Stupid stupid Jordan!" he said, banging his own head with his fist.

"Well, you better tell us what their plans are..." said Skylar. "Or else..."

Usually, the Office Tribe were not a particularly intimidating bunch, being comprised mostly of short people, but they were pissed off, and Jordan from Riverun was an idiot, so he spilled the beans immediately and told them everything he knew.

Meanwhile, Kitchen Tribe had all piled into the Viking Pontoon and were sailing it up the river. They were passing Blueberry Rock, and stopped because someone was standing at the top of it.

"Look!" pointed Gaston whose eyesight was as accurate as a hawk, or so he claimed.

"Is that...Lucy!?" said panicky Kat.

"It is me!" cried Lucy from the top of the rock. "Turn back! It's a tr—" Suddenly, she tumbled forwards off the cliff. Someone had pushed her!

This wouldn't be such a big deal in real life, but in this story Blueberry is a monstrous towering cliffface higher than a mountain and nobody could ever survive the deadly plummet. Lucy's scream echoed across the water, until she landed with a big splash. She had just enough time to feel her poor shoulder pop out for approximately the 17th time that year before she slipped out of this world and joined a few of the other Owlies in the afterlife...

Nobody questioned the logic of how she somehow went from Butchers Knife to Blueberry in the space of a single chapter, but that is yet another mystery that may or may not be explained before the end...

CHAPTER THIRTY-EIGHT

The next rapid of the day for Guide Tribe was Hair, named after the troll who lived on it. Remember those troll things from the 90s with the funny colourful hair? Yeah, its named after that. Now, getting past the troll was a simple matter of rocking out your best air guitar solo as you passed by his judgmental gaze. Owlies were notoriously good at this task.

None more so than Straun, who woke up every day with the assumption that he was starring in his own action movie. He had the looks at least, appearing to be some sort of freakish hybrid of Tom Cruise and Brad Pitt. However, Straun had one fatal weakness, which became apparent as he began his mighty guitar solo on his spear.

Without warning, he fumbled the spear and burst into uncontrollable tears.

"What's wrong!?" cried one of his clients, suddenly worried that the troll might eat them if Straun didn't pull his shit together in the next 3 seconds.

"Oh, I don't know," Straun blubbered. "There must be a puppy nearby. It's the only explanation."

Sure enough, a puppy had indeed come to visit Owl Clan that day. She loped in on her oversized puppy paws and bounded around the seemingly abandoned Clan grounds. Since everyone was out either hunting sea monsters, interrogating murderous spies or paddling down the river, it was left to Bootstrap Vinnie to witness her cuteness.

He descended from the ceiling of the office and cooed at the puppy, feeding her a snack and petting her fluffy head.

"Woof!" said the puppy in thanks.

Then she bounded outside and left, without another word. For a brief moment, the sun seemed to shine brighter and the spirits of every member of Owl Clan was lifted, even if they had no idea why.

Then the puppy was gone, and a cloud moved back in to cover the sun, blanketing the river in shadow.

It was a fitting change of atmosphere, because after Hair was the greatest challenge the Owl Clan had ever faced.

Looming up over the horizon roared the mighty Coliseum...

CHAPTER THIRTY-NINE

Aleisha and Colin were the next to go. Their air-guitar strumming just wasn't up to scratch, and the Hair troll was not impressed. He reached out with a surprisingly long arm and grabbed Colin around his waist, and boomed "ANY LAST WORDS?"

Colin shrugged. "Nah."

And the Troll bit off his head.

Aleisha saw all of this happen, and began to strum her spear extra hard, hoping the troll wouldn't notice that she was actually moving really, really, REALLY slowly... She wasn't able to move more than a snail's pace at the best of times, particularly when eating a meal. Sure enough, the troll noticed, and shook his head in disappointment. He reached out towards her with a big groping hand.

"No!" cried Aleisha. Then, in a desperate attempt to convince the troll not to eat her, she tore off her clothes and streaked up and down her boat, letting the troll see everything. This was her signature move, the one she'd used to secure Gwyn on a prom date. Would the troll be impressed, though?

"Sorry little hooman," said the troll. "But me no like melons. Me prefer sausage." He picked her up and swallowed her in a single gulp.

"He ate them!" yelled Fraser, frantically paddling with all his might, barking at his crew to push on. "Hard forwards! Go! Paddle you lazy dingos!"

He was so intent on paddling away from the troll that he forgot what was approaching. Ahead, water churned and raged, a mighty wave called Kahuna belched upwards into the air, a monstrous wall of churning water.

Fraser took one look at Coliseum, and his boat just flipped over. He wasn't even at the reactionary, but the fear simply took hold and Fraser lost control of his raft. Every one of his clients spilled into the water and were sucked downriver towards the maw of doom...

CHAPTER FORTY

Kitchen Tribe made it as far as Muskrat without seeing any hint of a fish, never mind a sea monster. They had no choice but to carry on upstream, in search of something to hunt for dinner. They all took up an oar and paddled hard, driving the pontoon up through the rapids.

Liam and Gaston were in the crow's nest, keeping a lookout. The muppets were always getting into trouble, and it was surprising they were given any responsibilities at all. Right now, they looked down at their Tribe paddling the longboat, and Liam decided now would be a good time to give them some encouragement.

"Row, you pussies!" he shouted. "Here, let me give you some sick gangsta choons!" He put on his favourite album, S Club 7, and blasted it down at his crew.

Gaston dozed off. He fell asleep next to the signal fire. He didn't even notice when the fire caught on his pants, and then his hair. He just sort of grunted incoherently saying "It's fine, let me sleep." It wasn't fine. Not at all.

As the Kitchen Tribe pontoon billowed black smoke into the air, the rafters up at Coliseum saw the signal and started to panic.

"The feast pontoon is in danger!" cried Naomi. She glanced at Coliseum and growled, "Let's get this done." She turned to her clients, a family of five, including two preschoolers. "Are you guys ready for the ride of your life?" she said menacingly, giving the toddlers a mean frown. "You better be! This is Coliseum, the nastiest rapid on the Ottawa. She will eat you, chew you up and spit you back out in seven pieces if you don't pay attention to what I have to say right now..." The toddlers started to cry.

Over in Imma's boat, a similar speech was happening. "Seriously, guys, just please, if you remember anything today, just paddle!" she explained desperately. "And if you do happen to fall out, which is actually rather likely, I want you to—"

"SWIM RIGHT!" said Tanner. "For the love of God, just swim—"

"That way!" said Oli, pointing vigorously. "Forget about your paddle, forget about your wife, forget about your—"

"...big balls," said Ben. "That's what you need to get through this, just like me." He winked at a pretty viking sitting at the back of his raft.

"Yargh, me matey's, man yer rudders!" barked Pirate Gwyn. "I'm going in!"

Gwyn steered his raft into the approach. He lined himself up with the reactionary and bounced off it perfectly. Now, he was steering straight towards Kahuna. This was it. This was do or die. What sort of mood was she in today? Would she surge, or would she snooze?

Gwyn's raft ploughed into it head on. His line was perfect, but it mattered not. Kahuna roared, and Gwyn's raft soared. Up and over it went, spilling everyone into the churning waters.

Except...

Somehow, against all the odds, as the rest of Guide Tribe looked on in awe, they saw that Gwyn was still clinging to his raft...by his ankles. Gwyn was not just a pirate, you see. He was a Ninja Pirate.

CHAPTER FORTY-ONE

"So, what did Jordan tell us after you interrogated him?" asked Kaitlyn to Office Tribe when they returned from the cornfield.

"You'll never believe it," said Mic-Mack. "WT are so pissed at me for stealing their stupid sign, they have declared full on Clan War with us. They are going to make an all-out rear assault on our Ghetto in about twenty minutes."

"Well, then what are we standing around here for?" said Skylar.

"Regan had the right idea," said Marianne. "Her last words before being skewered were 'Let's set some traps!'"

And so they began to prepare for war. With the help of Flemmingo, who had been building camp fires since the day he had been born, they piled the Ghetto fire with extra wood, dug beer pits all across the floor and covered them with leaves to hide them. They setup tripwires out of flip lines, catapults out of paddles, and Kaitlyn gave Charlie the cat a prep-talk...

"When those WT idiots come, you do that cat thing where you slip between their legs and act all cute okay? Then bite their ankles and they'll fall into our fire."

This was a bit extreme for Kaitlyn, who had a reputation for being a sensible manager with a calm disposition. But deep down, she was constantly holding back her primal urge for chaos and destruction. A war with WT would bring out her true colours...

CHAPTER FORTY-TWO

A darkness was descending over the Ottawa. A general feeling of closure hung in the air, as 'The End' approached...

The vikings of Guide Tribe were lined up at the top of Coliseum, after witnessing both Fraser and Gwyn's carnage, everyone feared who would be next.

It was Marc's job to capture all of this anxiety in art form, and he stood on the bow of his pedal-boat, carving a picture into his stone tablet. He worked skilfully, etching out the moody images of all the Owl Clan boats as they waited in grim silence at the top of the raging rapid. The surviving clients looked nervous, and the guides even more so. They all knew what was waiting for them below the ridge of water.

Marc couldn't help but chuckle to himself. Watching clients tumble out of their boats and frantically swim through rapids was a highlight of his day.

Then he looked across, and saw Scottish Scott, his ultimate rival.

"Why you..." Marc growled to himself.

Scott had found a superior position on a rock with a perfect view of Kahuna. He was busy carving away at his stone tablet, creating a piece of art so realistic that even the most tight-arsed client would not be able to resist paying for a copy.

Then he too spotted Marc, his ultimate rival.

"Why you…" he growled.

The pair of Viking Artists locked eyes, glaring at each other with disdain. Only one of them could emerge from this summer as the Viking Artist Champion, and neither one would accept defeat…

Then there was movement. A raft left the pack, and drifted into the current. Straun was at the helm. He stood in his hero pose at the back of the raft and ordered his scared-looking crew to drive forwards. They accelerated, aiming straight at the reactionary.

A good start, he thought to himself, lining himself up with Kahuna. "Hard forwards!" he called.

But his clients froze in terror. Nobody was paddling.

"No!" Straun cried, feeling his boat slow. "What did I tell you! You have to spear the dragon!!!" He dived forwards over the thwarts and took up position at the bow, as the massive wave bore down on them.

Straun lifted his spear above his head, primed to thrust it into the heart of the wave... but then a paralysing terror swept through him, as he stared straight into the eye... of an actual dragon.

Yes, the reason Coliseum is so big, is because the Fourth and Final River God lay at the bottom of the rapid. He was a scaly monstrosity of epic proportions, and the Guide Tribe of Owl Clan had just awoken the sleeping dragon.

This wasn't going to end well.

CHAPTER FORTY-THREE

The dragon stood up. When it did, Kahuna disappeared. So that's what really happens at low level Coliseum...

It hefted itself up onto all fours, and stretched its long neck, river water pouring off its back like a waterfall. Straun's raft bumped up against its leg and became stuck. Every other raft stopped paddling, but the current pulled them onward towards the gigantic scaly beast. A chorus of screams filled the air, and it was impossible to tell who was loudest - the punters or Guide Tribe.

Then came another sound. A thunderous warcry from downriver. The dragon turned its head to see where it was coming from. The Viking Pontoon had arrived, carrying Kitchen Tribe!

"There's our dinner!" cried Erin, pointing a whisk at the dragon. "Kitchen Tribe, WITH ME!"

Erin charged towards the front of the longboat armed with the cooking utensil, ran up the prow and leaped off it straight at the dragon. In mid-air, the dragon calmly reached down and plucked her out of the air, catching Erin by the apron in her giant teeth. She flipped Erin into the air, sending her into a spiral. Then with a small fiery belch, she burped a fireball upwards, instantly toasting Erin into a medium-rare bit of steak and then swallowed her whole.

In one dragon gulp, Erin's tyrannical reign over

Kitchen Tribe had finally come to an end. It was now up to Bombaci to lead them to victory... or die trying.

Farewell Erin. See you in Valhalla. (Fernie)

CHAPTER FORTY-FOUR

Oli saw an opportunity. He'd waited patiently for his time to shine in the story, and since Matt had no other ideas for what to write for him, Oli pulled out a skateboard, ran along the edge of his boat and ollied right onto the dragon's tail. He skateboarded up its back, weaving in and out of her spiny spikes. The dragon turned her head and leaned around trying to bite him, but he was too fast!

Her giant splashing legs flipped Straun's boat over, toppling him and all of his clients into the river. Straun tried to scream but too many briefings and morning rally-calls had left him with basically no voice and he just fell in gurgling.

Gwyn bellowed a command to drive the rest of the trip forwards, intending to raft past the dragon while it was distracted.

Oli's distraction almost worked. He skateboarded right up and over the dragons head, hunkered to leap off its nose and prepared to pull off some kinda badass trick that would surely dazzle the dragon and make it realise that she could not possibly win a fight against the mighty Owl Clan... But then Oli wondered what the hell he was doing riding a skateboard along a dragon, and remembered that he was a paddler, not a skateboarder, so he just sort of flopped off the dragon's head and tumbled head over heels right into her line of fire.

Time froze for a moment. The dragon's jaws were open wide as she took aim, a fiery glow radiating from the depths of her mouth. Every member of Guide Tribe found themselves gaping in horror down her throat, which was aiming straight at them. Oli was falling through the air in front of her. And any moment now, the entire rafting trip was about to take a torrent of angry dragon breath to the face.

Not everyone would survive. Particularly those leaving on Monday.

But at exactly the same time, back at base...

CHAPTER FORTY-FIVE

WT Clan attacked from the most strategic position their chimp-like minds could come up with – straight down the main road.

A swarm of them came armed with axes, clubs, spears and broken paddles. At the pig path they split up. Some entered the path headed towards the pig pen while the rest carried on, intending to assault Dirk and Claudia's cottage.

Sid was feeding the pigs when they showed up. She wasn't interested in hunting a sea monster for dinner, so when Kitchen Tribe had ventured forth she sneakily stayed behind to hang out with her best friends, the cute piggies.

"Who's that!?" growled a WT viking that looked a lot like a weasel.

Sid scowled at them. "Go away! You don't live here."

"Look how small she is!" laughed one of the others, who smelled like a skunk.

"I will fight you…" Sid warned. "I'll fight all of you if I have to."

The WT monkeys all laughed, and strode forward, not heeding Sidney's threat because they assumed she wouldn't be able to hurt a fly.

That was their undoing.

Sid went into a blind rage. Her fists flew this way and that in a shocking display of violence, entirely unexpected from someone who lives on tofu and salad. She destroyed the raiding party, leaving blood and viscera strewn all across the bushes, the trees, and several severed limbs found their way into the pig pen.

At one point however, Sid took an unfortunate axe to the face. She didn't notice until the brawl was over, but then it became rather impossible to ignore.

"Okay, I'm out," she said, and collapsed down dead.

CHAPTER FORTY-SIX
(mildly intoxicated but can't remember the occasion)

Panicky Kat saw it all go down. She was running around the pontoon boat shrieking about missing sausages, and she just couldn't handle it, and suddenly a huge bolt of lightning streaked out of the sky and fried her bones.

Have a break, Kat. Have a Kit Kat.

In Valhalla.

CHAPTER FORTY-SEVEN

The remainder of the WT raiding party paused along the road when they heard their fellow clanmates screaming and dying somewhere behind them. All but one of them abandoned their advance on the cottage, and retreated to investigate the noises. Only Kawolski continued. He wanted blood tonight... Dirk's.

The rest arrived at the pig pen and crapped their pants. They passed the remains of their clanmates and Sidney's corpse and continued onwards, heading for the Ghetto.

They entered the snake pit and saw two people lying naked in the grass, on top of each other. They may have been having sex.

"Yeah! 3 points for those guys!" cried one of the WT hooligans, and others started clapping. They were used to seeing sights like this, but it was less common at Owl Clan. The raiders charged towards the couple and that's when they triggered the traps.

"AAAAGH!" cried one as he fell into a spike-filled hidden beer pit.

"AAAEEEIII!" screamed two others when they set off a bear trap.

"Attack!" came a shout from the trees, and Office Tribe emerged in full battle gear, swinging their axes and going berserk.

A petrol bomb came flying out of the woods, spears began to fly, and Charlie the cat leapt out of a tree and went for the eyes. Of everyone.

Marianne, Margaret and Mic-Mack chopped off heads, legs and arms as the flames spread around the campfire, jumping from Aleisha's platform and then to Ben's. Soon, the entire Snake Pit was on fire, as the battle raged within.

It was going so well until Skylar took a spear through the belly... "Nooooo!" she wailed, reaching for the sky in a dramatic pose. She stumbled backwards and tripped over someone's leg. It belonged to Taylor, who was still lying on top of Nick Who Rafts Often. The two of them hadn't noticed the fighting and were still sprawled out in the grass. Skylar fell backwards and the spear sticking out of her back went through both of them, pinning them all to the ground in some sick, and admittedly unlikely trio of dead Owlies.

Skylar, Nick and Taylor found themselves at the gates of Valhalla, which were thumping to the beats of 'Let's Get Retarded' by the Black Eyed Peas.

"Well, I guess we live here now," said Skylar. And they all walked in.

CHAPTER FORTY-EIGHT

Are you ready for this? I don't think you are. Those of a nervous disposition may want to put down their phones (or copy of this book) and walk away. Seriously.

Are you still here? Do you know what you're getting into? We are approaching the Grand Climax of this ridiculous story, and things are about to get biblically messy.

This is your last warning.

The end is nigh, my friends...

Matt crept out of the bushes at the side of Coliseum, and caught sight of the enormous dragon. It looked mean, angry, and definitely capable of being a criminal, so he assumed it must be Eddie.

"I found you!" he cried, pointing at the dragon.

A splash leapt up from around the dragon's feet as Oli landed in the river. And a heartbeat later, the dragon belched the biggest fireball anyone had ever seen straight into the heart of Guide Tribe and their rafts.

Straun's puppy tears evaporated and then he was melted instantly.

Gwyn used his ninja skills to leap out of the way and ducked under water as the flames roared above his head. Squid followed him, falling out of his boat just in the nick of time. Poor Imma was turned into burnt toast as the dragonfire swept on, incinerating her raft and all of her clients.

The flames boiled the river, turning it into a nice hot bath-like temperature, which would be very pleasant under other circumstances.

"Attack!" roared Big Ben, pointing his wooden spoon towards the dragon, before charging in. He was joined by the Ozzie Carnage Contenders, as Mitch chucked spears at it with the accuracy of an Australian cricketer, Tim launched his rope around the dragon's horn and began to climb up it, and Fraser... actually, Fraser was still floundering around in the river at this point.

The dragon went crazy, snapping and biting everything in its way. It munched Aiden's leg off.

"Aaaagh!" he cried, clutching his bloody stump. "It's all right, I can still work weekends!"

But the dragon cared not. She spotted Holly, another supposed weekender and squashed her with a giant scaly claw. Then the dragon leaned down and chomped at the dancing Gus, who disappeared down her gullet in a flash of tartan. He may not have been ready to go to Valhalla, but he'd spent so long at MKC the last few weeks that everyone had forgotten what he even looked like, anyway.

Evelyn cried out, devastated at losing a fellow dancer, and she decided to go out in style, by pulling a fancy ballerina pose on the prow of her raft, just as the dragon whipped her tail and sent Evelyn soaring into the stratosphere.

Kitchen Tribe began to hurl knives, forks and spoons at the dragon in a desperate attempt to get its attention. It worked. The dragon turned around and spat another burst of fire across their deck.

Everyone ducked down out of the way...except

Hannah. She disappeared in a puff of smoke. The flames leapt out of the Longboat Pontoon and surged into the forest on the riverbank, incinerating dozens of trees.

Paige was furious about this. "NOT MY TREEEES!" she bellowed, and leapt off the boat, swam to shore, and began frantically replanting seeds, because that's what she does.

The dragon turned around again as Guide Tribe prepared themselves for another bit of carnage.

Meanwhile, The Battle of the Snake Pit was still in full swing. Office and Ops Tribe were fighting off the WT invaders with reckless ferocity.

Flemmingo had taken up his seat on the Goat-Walkder, a deadly machine normally used to cut grass, but now he was using it to run over WT warriors, chopping them into pieces, and spraying the Ghetto with their blood.

Then he hit a rock.

The wagon stopped so abruptly that he was chucked forwards out of the seat and landed on the grass. The goats kept pulling at the wagon and jerked it free, running Flemmingo over, sucking him into the deadly blades and putting an end to his salty complaining once and for all.

None were more valiant than Mic-Mack and Kaitlyn, the deadly duo who had been friends since basically childbirth, and managed to murder twelve of the hooligans as they led them into the Main Ghetto. Mic-Mack taunted a group of them with the stolen sign, waving it above her head, yelling "Come and get it ya filthy animals!" Then she chucked it into the Ghetto Fire. As six WT axemen dived into the mound of dead branches and wooden pallets, Kaitlyn casually tossed a whiskey bottle into it, and Mic-Mack threw in a match.

KABOOM.

They cackled in glee together as they watched the fire burn.

Then someone pushed them both in the back and they fell in themselves. They joined the ever-growing list of Owl Clan party members in Valhalla.

Mic-Mack went straight to the afterlife bar and ordered a drink, gazing around at the scenery. "My god, it's just like Rafters!" she declared with a happy grin.

She sat back, sipping her drink, waiting for more Owlies to show up. She wouldn't have to wait long...

CHAPTER FORTY-NINE

The penultimate chapter was upon us. It started with a rude knock on the cottage door.

Dirk looked up from his cup of tea, and got up to see who it was. Before he reached the door though, someone booted it so hard from the other side that it flew off the hinges and crashed to the floor.

"You!" Dirk bellowed, throwing his cup away, and unsheathing his double-bladed battleaxe.

"Yes, it's me, your arch nemesis," said Kawoslski. "For too long have you ruled this river. Now it is time to give up, and hand over the--"

Dirk chopped off his head. It bounced down the steps, and Dirk walked back to make himself another cup of tea.

Back at Coliseum, the dragon roared, and stamped its feet and spat fiery death on Guide and Kitchen Tribe. The Longboat Pontoon was aflame, billowing huge plumes of choking black smoke into the sky.

"Abandon ship!" screamed Bombaci, tossing his spatula aside and throwing himself overboard.

The dragon heard him yell, and inhaled a deep breath, preparing another fire blast.

Most of Kitchen Tribe made it out, but Nolan. Nolan... Nolan stayed on the river. He couldn't abandon his ship, and he clung to the steering wheel with white knuckles, staring the dragon in the face as she exhaled. The fiery inferno engulfed the Viking

Pontoon, utterly destroying it in a gigantic explosion of splintery, charred wood and Nolan's bones.

"Swim to me!" cried Paige waving frantically from the riverbank.

What few remained of Kitchen Tribe all swam away from the burning wreckage of their boat and scrambled up onto shore. Except Heroux. She had somehow emerged from the burning boat in-tact, and riding her bike. Now, she was pedaling so fast that she was skimming across the water's surface like Jesus-on-a-bike and she raced towards Guide Tribe with a determined look on her face.

"Dylan!" she cried. She sped towards her beloved's boat, and as she passed by, he jumped onto the back, and they both shot away from the dragon up the river. The dragon turned and followed them with her gaze, drawing in another breath.

The rest of Guide Tribe took advantage of the distraction and hurled everything they had at the beast. They bombarded her with spears and stones and wooden spoons, drawing blood in multiple places. The dragon howled in pain, and spewed a deadly blast of fire that incinerated heroic Heroux and Dylan. Their bike carried on for a little while before falling over with a splash.

"AAAAROOOOOGHHH!" came a thunderous warshout, and everyone looked up to see T-Roy and Ariana leaping from the Coliseum platform and landed on the dragon's back with daggers digging into her flesh. They swiped and slashed and tore chunks out of her before the dragon unfurled its pair of mighty wings and took to the sky. Tim let go of the rope he was dangling to and fell into the river, as the dragon carried the Hobbits into the air.

Guide Tribe kept throwing things at her, most missing their mark, because throwing things with accuracy wasn't exactly their strong suit (Matt was basing this off of their practice throws back at base).

"This doesn't look good," said Steff, making her debut appearance in the story, and deciding that it would be best if she just stayed out of everyone's way. Fighting dragons and stuff seemed like a lot of effort...

Then suddenly, out of the darkening sky came a flash of lightning. And with it, the sound of whooshing, as something big and fast fell towards the dragon.

It was Thor! He smote the dragon with his hammer, and she recoiled, thrashing her wings. She lost control and tumbled out of the sky, plummeting straight down.

Ben and Mitch looked up and gulped. "Oh, bollocks," said Ben.

"Yup, nice knowin' ya mate," said Mitch.

The dragon spun and landed on her back. T-Roy and Ariana made eye contact with Ben and Mitch for a brief second before all of them were splatted beneath the weight of the gigantic monster.

Thor's hammer suddenly landed in the water with a splash a moment later and sunk to the bottom of the riverbed. The man himself had disappeared quietly without saying goodbye...

A nearby figure could be seen swimming down underwater to retrieve the hammer, but who could it be? Only Thor could wield the hammer, everyone knew that. Only someone truly worthy could possibly stand a chance of using it for themselves...

But then, a hand flew out of the water, clutching

the hammer.

"Fraser!" cried Kitchen Tribe from the shore.

Yes. Fraser was worthy. He floated up out of the water, suddenly able to fly, because of all the people in Guide Tribe, he was The Chosen One. The one who had been named King. He was the Carnage King, and right now, there was a lot of carnage going on.

"It's time to put an end to this," he declared bravely. And he took up the hammer, staring the dragon in the face. Because you see, no matter how many times Fraser had been beaten, battered and bruised... he never gave up. He would always keep coming back for more. That's the definition of bravery. And if there was to be some kind of moral to take away from this ridiculous, stupid story, then let it be that.

Fraser smacked the dragon around the head with the hammer. She fell over dead and returned to her place in the river, at the bed of Kahuna. And there she remained for the next thousand years.

THE FINAL CHAPTER

With the defeat of their leader, the few survivors of WT Clan retreated back to the filthy pit from whence they came. Owl Clan were victorious.

Office Tribe let out a mighty cheer which echoed across the valley. They left the Ghetto burning as they made their way to the docks.

Kitchen Tribe and Guide Tribe were being pulled along by a rope behind Marc's pedal-boat. Only Matt remained of Ops Tribe. In fact, there were very few survivors, but those that had made it would surely have some stories to tell, and memories to keep for the rest of their lives. Nothing creates a stronger friendship than a near-death experience... or a season on the Ottawa. They arrived at the beach, and slowly emerged dripping and bleeding and clutching each other for support.

But they were also smiling.

"We did it!" cried Ferrari, pumping his fist in the air.

"We survived!" shouted Bombaci, high-fiving his Kitchen comrades.

Bootstrap Vinnie, for the first time in several hundred years, left the office and wandered down to the beach to join the celebrations. "Victory!" he declared.

Dirk arrived then, dragging behind him a large crate. "Well done everyone. I'm proud of you all." He turned to the crate, and kicked it open. Inside were an assortment of musical instruments, including a big drum and a bunch of horns, plus an enormous wooden barrel of beer.

"BEACH PARTY!!!" they yelled.

And the survivors of Owl Clan broke into song and dance.

Far above, beyond the boundary of the universe in Valhalla, the missing but not forgotten members of Owl Clan were looking down, raising their own glasses and cheering their fellow clanmates.

Everyone in Owl Clan would soon go their separate ways. The summer was over, and winter was fast approaching. A small group would travel west, to the fabled mountain town of Fernie. Others were returning to the Land of Oz, where it was always summer, and people walked upsidedown. But most were returning to school, to learn the ways of something called 'adulthood'. It was tedious and dull, but it had to be done.

Wherever each individual might be going, there would always be the summer of 2017 that connected them. The summer of the Great Cupcake Debate. The summer of Gaston's Quest for Self-Improvement. The summer of Never-Ending High Water Coliseum. The summer of River Gods, River Muppets, Ghetto Queens, Carnage Kings, and The Arrival of Unlimited WiFi.

The sun set on summer, and an autumn moon rose into the sky over Owl Clan. The tribes danced long into the night, finally enjoying a lifelong goal of having an actual party on the beach, while their clanmates did the same up in Valhalla. Perhaps one day, they would all meet again.

THE END

A NOTE FROM THE AUTHOR

Well what a load of nonsense that was.

I must thank all of the friends (and enemies) I made at Owl Rafting during what has probably been the best summer of my life. If you aren't one of them, and yet are somehow reading this book, I can only apologise… You won't understand any of the references and in-jokes that are littered throughout this half-arsed attempt at a story.

Still, I had immense fun writing it. I suppose I should apologise to all of the friends (and enemies) that I made at Owl Rafting too, because I gave no forewarning that I was about to spend 2 solid months taking the piss out of them and posting it in our Facebook group for everyone else to see.

I hope that this finished book serves as a suitable apology / memento of our time together. I meant what I said about this being the best summer I've ever had… Thank you, each and every one of you.

Especially you, Dirk and Claudia. Keep doing what you do, for as long as you can. You're both awesome.

I'm now off to spend time in my more natural habitat… a snowy mountain. Farewell, for now.

M A Clarke,
September 2017

ABOUT THE AUTHOR

M A Clarke is a 31 year old geek from England who grew up watching cartoons, animating his own cartoons, and playing video games.

He recently decided to explore the world and see what life was like away from a screen. Rather ironically, travelling inspired him to sit in front of a screen and write his first novel, *Lunaria*. Then he did it again and wrote *The Horizon Conspiracy*.

He has a dangerous addiction to Wispa chocolate bars (only available in England) and also loves mountains, dogs, dinosaurs and space.

You might like his website: www.mattclarke.co.uk